The Luck Child

BY GAYNOR CHAPMAN

Based on a story of the Brothers Grimm

ATHENEUM   1968   NEW YORK

One day a long time ago a poor woman gave birth to a fine baby boy. His eyes were especially beautiful. One of them was deep brown, the other as pale blue as the sky at a winter's dawn. Everyone in the village came to admire the poor woman's boy.

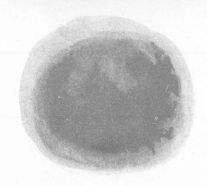

The Court Astrologer heard about the baby and predicted by the strangeness of the boy's eyes that he would be a Luck Child, one whom good fortune would always follow, and who would grow up to marry the King's daughter.

When the King heard of this prediction he was very alarmed and set off for the village where the baby had been born. He was a bad king, much disliked by his people, and he determined in his cold heart to destroy the Luck Child. He went to the poor woman's cottage, disguised as a traveller, and said, "Let me look after this child, my good woman. I will see that he has all the best in life."

The woman, believing that good fortune had already
begun for her Luck Child, allowed the traveller to take

away her baby, though she wept at the loss and wondered
when she would see her child again.

The wicked King went next to the village carpenter and tossed him a golden coin. "Make me a box to carry the Luck Child on my horse," he ordered. The King rode off with the box strapped behind him. As he passed the cottage of the poor woman he raised his hat in farewell. "Good fortune will follow your Luck Child," he said.

But once out of sight of the village, the King galloped to the nearest river. "Someone must have cast a spell on this child that he should have one brown and one blue eye," he said. "He is too poor and humble to marry my beautiful Princess." Then he unstrapped the box and hurled it into the deep, fast-flowing waters. But good fortune followed the Luck Child. The box fell in the river and floated safely as far as a mill. The miller's wife saw it and called to her husband.

"A treasure chest! Quick, help me catch it!" When they saw the Luck Child lying inside the box, the miller's wife, who had no child of her own, said, "Oh, what a wonderful treasure! We will bring up this beautiful boy as our own."

Sixteen years passed, and the Luck Child grew up into a handsome and strong youth. One day a wild boar came

past the mill, followed by a pack of hounds, and then a
group of grandly dressed huntsmen.

One of them demanded of the miller, "Where did the wild boar go?" The miller recognised the King and bowed low. The King saw a handsome youth standing beside the miller, and realised, from the one brown and one blue eye, that it was the Luck Child he had tried to

drown years before. The King dismounted, pretending friendliness for the miller and the youth. "Is this fine boy your son?" he asked. "No, Your Majesty, he is a foundling. Sixteen years ago he floated down this river in a box and we rescued him."

The King smiled, but in his cold heart he was plotting again to destroy the Luck Child who would soon be of an age to marry his beautiful daughter. "If he can run fast, I will pay him a golden coin to take a message to the Queen." The King wrote a letter, sealed it with the royal seal, handed it to the boy, and galloped away to rejoin the hunt.

The boy ran off, pleased to be carrying such a grand message. But to reach the royal palace he had to go through a great forest. There he missed a turning and soon found that he was lost. As dusk fell, he caught sight of a light in a cottage and knocked on the door. A woman opened it. "Poor lad," she said, "you look tired out."

She gave the boy a hot supper, after which he lay down and at once fell fast asleep. Moments later, there was a great noise at the door and three men came in. They were in high spirits, as well they might be, for they were

robbers and carried bundles full of booty. "Mother," they called out loudly, "look what we have!" "Hush!" said the woman quietly to her sons. "There is a poor boy asleep over there."

After their supper the three robbers went and looked at the boy, and from habit felt in his pockets. They put back the one gold coin for he seemed so poor, but looked more curiously at the letter with the gold seal on it. One of the three robbers broke the seal and read aloud the letter from the King. "To Her Majesty the Queen," it ran. "A lad will bring this letter to you. He is a danger to our Princess. Have him killed at once."

The robbers were sorry for the boy. They wrote a different letter, put it in an envelope and carefully replaced the royal seal. The next morning the woman sent the boy on his way, and he soon reached the royal palace where he presented the letter to the Queen. With a shaking voice the Queen read the letter aloud to her

courtiers: "I have been mortally wounded in a hunting accident. This fine lad tended my injuries and as a reward it is my dying wish that he should marry the Princess and become King."

The humble boy and the beautiful Princess fell in love the moment they met.

and the crowning of the new King and Queen.

Hundreds of people came from far and near to wave and cheer, for they were happy to have a good king at last. Among them were the miller and his wife, the Court Astrologer, and the poor woman whose Luck Child had indeed had the good fortune predicted for him.

Soon after the coronation, the bad King returned, tired and mud-spattered, from his hunting trip.

Imagine his rage when he found that he was no longer King, that the humble boy he had tried twice to kill was now on the throne in his place, and that he had, after all, married the beautiful Princess. "What have you been doing while I have been away?" he demanded furiously.

"We thought you were dead, and we were only following your last wishes," answered his wife, showing the King the letter written by the robbers.

The old bad King now saw that his own wickedness had brought about his downfall. So when the new King and the new Queen offered him a house in the palace grounds, he accepted with good grace. In his old age he became a better man than he had been as King.